The Candlelight Gifts

A Keeper's Tale

J.A. Andrews

For everyone who ever thought,
"I wonder what happened to Douglon and Rass
and aaaaallllll those baby elves?"

Happy Reading
-Janice

1

THE FIRST GIFTS

RASS LAY in her small clearing, her back nestled down into the crunchy brown grass. The only cloud above her in the blue sky was from her own breath, hovering for a moment before fading into the chilly afternoon.

Even now, at the lowest point in the year when the grass had run out of the power to stay green, when it had hollowed out and dried out until any step or strong wind would break it, the roots were still alive.

But those were fading too. It was a fortnight until midwinter, and soon lying in the grass wouldn't be enough to keep her warm.

Rass shifted, pulling her skinny knees up, the crunch of the grass mirroring her own brittleness. She held up one hand, her fingers bony and thin against the sky. Fragile looking.

Delicate, little snip, Douglon would correct her, but his brow would crease with that fatherly worry he was never able to hide at this time of year.

She lowered her hand. It wasn't that winter was hard—it was just another season, part of the cycle. The grass grew in the spring, thrived in the summer, faded in the autumn, and waited through the winter.

And so Rass, and all the other grass elves who lived far away across the mountains, would fade and wait with it.

Rass would wait here in the Lumen Greenwood with her new family.

An unusual family to be sure: forty-six two-year-old tree elves, the wild little siblings Rass had never known she needed, and Uncle Douglon, the dwarf who managed to take care of them all. He'd be returning from a trip to the human capital today, coming back to the home that was as odd for a dwarf as it was for a grass elf. She listened for his heavy footsteps but heard nothing.

She sighed. The forest always felt a little unmoored without Douglon's steadiness.

The sky above Rass was framed by vibrant trees. Some were pines bristling with soft needles; some flaunted leaves still shimmering with their autumn colors, even though it was months past when the trees outside the Greenwood would have lost their grip on such finery.

It would be nice if the Greenwood would protect the grass in the same way, but the tree elves—and the forest itself—were primarily obsessed with trees. They were nice trees, but still trees, and the weak point about trees, like so many other things, was that they weren't grass.

Rass's own personal grassland was rather small. It stretched merely a half-dozen paces in every direction before it was strangled out by the shadows of the woods. Grass continued throughout the forest floor, of course, but in the entire Greenwood, it was only lush here.

This was nothing like the Roven Sweep, where the grass spread endless and infinite across the hills, green or golden under the vast sky, taller than her head in the deep summer. A sea of grass she could slip through, burrow into, lose herself in.

Here, the grasses were short, never reaching more than halfway to her knees. She didn't need this clearing. There was always grass somewhere, even if only in little tufts here and there. But the extravagance of an entire glade was luxurious, and she loved nothing more than lying here, taking a short break from the maelstrom of the baby tree elves.

She let her mind wander along the roots, finding worms and grubs digging in the earth or insects scurrying over it. Farther out into the forest, she felt tiny tree elf feet dropping into the grass occasionally before jumping back up on a tree.

A slight commotion rustled from somewhere down the nearest path, and she reached out through the grass to see who it was.

She needn't have bothered. The grass told her of the heavy tread of Douglon's dwarvish boots at the same time as a small voice squealed from a treetop.

"Uncle Doug Doug!" Avina shrieked.

Rass sat up in time to see a bright metallic streak leap out of a tree and slam into the dwarf. Douglon grunted and staggered slightly but reached up to hug the tree elf. She was barely half his size, her delicate skin glittering with coppery sparkles, her long hair richer and brighter, glowing like the burnished copper jewelry Rass had seen among the dwarves.

A smile peeked out from behind Douglon's beard. His dark red hair looked almost brown by comparison to her brightness. "Hello, Avina. I missed you too. You'll be happy to know I brought gifts."

Rass pushed herself to her feet, the motion taking a bit of effort, and started toward him. "Welcome home, Uncle."

His smile faltered just for a heartbeat when his eyes caught on the sharp angle of her shoulders under her tunic, and then he forced it wider again. "Hullo, snip. Are you keeping warm enough?"

She nodded as he strode into her clearing, and she threw her arms around his waist. She'd never understood the way humans and dwarves seemed to love leather until Douglon had carried her through those long, dark dwarven tunnels years ago, also carrying a strip of earth with grass on his back for days just so she'd have somewhere to sleep at night. She'd burrowed against his leather vest, his arms carrying her through it all, strong enough to hold back the entire mountain above her. And now, leather was one of her favorite smells. Not as good as a wide rustling grassland, but close.

He stepped back and squatted down, setting one hand gently on her shoulder, the worry she had been prepared for creeping into his eyes.

"I'm not going to break," she said.

He grunted in an unconvinced way. "Thin as a snip of grass. I can't wait for spring."

"Gifts?" Avina asked, tugging on the bag tossed over his back. Over the past two years, she'd established herself firmly as the leader of all the little tree elves.

"Yes, gifts." He slung the pack down to the ground and knelt next to it. "The humans exchange presents on Midwinter Day. They call them Candlelight Gifts and claim that giving gifts brightens the longest night of the year. Like the light of a candle flame in the darkness." He brought out a pouch of bright orange fabric and handed it to Avina. "That's from Sini."

She gave a squeal of delight and plopped down next to Douglon.

Rass nestled down into the grass too, leaning forward to peer into his bag as a second gift appeared, a large green bundle of woven fabric, bigger than her head. It looked like a wrapped blanket, held closed by a metal pin.

"For Rass," he said, "from Will."

Her fingers sank into the soft wool, her skin pale against the rich green. The pin was delicate and silver, shaped like a sheaf of grass.

Finally, Douglon pulled out a skinny package a bit longer than his hand. "And Alaric gave me something, which I saved to open with you two."

Avina's fingers were clenched around her package, and she stared at the two of them with wide eyes, barely containing herself.

"Go ahead," Douglon said.

Avina tore her pouch open and turned it upside down. A single acorn fell into her palm. "New tree!"

"New?" Rass asked.

Avina closed her eyes and wrapped her hand around it. "Different tree. Different leaves." Her eyes flew open. "Avina plant this!" She leapt up and raced to the nearest tree, scurrying up the trunk and leaping from branch to branch until she disappeared.

"I guess she likes it." Douglon looked after her fondly. "Open yours."

Rass unhooked the pin, and the bundle of wool tumbled apart in her lap.

Not a blanket. A cloak.

Rass ran her fingers over the woven wool. "It's soft as a cloud!"

"Will's not totally useless," Douglon said with an approving nod. "That should keep even you warm for the winter."

Rass stood and spread the cloak around her shoulders, clasping it at her neck with the pin. It wrapped around her, warm and heavy, and she drew it closer and beamed at him. "I love it. Tell Will to come visit so I can tell him."

"It fits you well." He turned to his own package and unwrapped a rectangular stone sitting on a wooden base. "Oooooh," he breathed. "A water stone!"

Rass leaned forward to see it better. It was an unremarkable piece of rock. Flat on all sides, not quite smooth, not quite bumpy. Too big for her to hold easily, but perfectly fit for Douglon's hands. "A what?"

"A kind of whetstone. A good one. Dwarven, I think. I wonder where he found this?" Douglon grabbed his axe off the outside of his pack where it hung when he traveled. He set it across his lap, his fingers trailing almost absently along the red flames that wrapped around the handle. They were carved into the wood, or maybe frozen around it—it was hard to tell—a gift to him from Ayda, the first elf he'd ever met. The color was stunning. A shimmering, rich, deep red that somehow embodied actual fire.

The axe head was something called stonesteel, a fact Douglon was quite proud of, even if Rass thought it looked like all the other metal things in the world.

Douglon took the whetstone and began to slide it along his axe blade, nodding slowly in approval. "This is fantastic."

"Do dwarves give gifts at Midwinter?"

He nodded, and a slight smile touched his cheek. "Just among their closest family and friends. Humans tend to lavish gifts on anyone they know, but dwarves focus on their closest loved ones."

His hands held the axe head with gentle familiarity, his brow creased in concentration.

"Do you miss them?" she asked quietly. "The dwarves?"

The whetstone moved smoothly along the blade as he glanced up at her. "There are things I miss, yes. But none of it as much as I miss my little elves when I'm away from the Greenwood."

Beside him, his pack still sat, full of his traveling gear. Her brow crinkled at the sight. "You didn't drop your pack off at the cottage?"

His hand paused, and he looked up to face her fully. "I need to run to Duncave for a bit. Shouldn't take long. I'll be back by Midwinter."

Her shoulders sank, and he grimaced.

"After that," he added quickly, "I should be here until spring. Can you make it another fortnight without me?"

She let out a snort. "I did survive winters before I met you."

"I know. But who will make you a fire if you need it?"

Rass shushed him and glanced into the trees. "Don't let Avina hear you! She lit the line of bushes near the stream yesterday. Don't give her any more ideas about fire."

He chuckled. "It's astonishing the Greenwood—the whole world—has survived the last two years." He looked at Rass, the fondness still in his eyes. "I'll be back as quick as I can."

Rass silenced the sigh that tried to sneak out of her and worked a smile onto her face. "We'll have a good dinner tonight before you go."

Douglon reached out and set his thick hand on her shoulder again. "I promise I'll hurry back. This is my favorite place in the world, you know."

She glanced around at the grass. "My clearing?"

He squeezed her gently and didn't quite hide the cloud in his expression at how thin her shoulder was. "With you and all my elves, little snip."

2

THE PLAN

Rass stood at the door of the low, stone cottage she shared with Douglon, watching him clomp away down the frosty trail until he turned a corner, out of sight. Avina leaned against her side, letting out a long sigh that hung in the air like a cloud in the early light.

Rass tightened her new cloak around her shoulders. "We should make Douglon a Candlelight Gift."

Avina nodded. "Lub Doug Doug."

"Yes, we love him. What do you think he would like?"

Avina looked up at her. "Tree!"

Rass laughed and looked around the strange bit of forest surrounding them. Douglon had named this the Nursery, chortling something about baby elves and growing trees.

Above them, bridges stretched between tall tree trunks, connecting dozens of treehouses and platforms and gathering rooms. The Greenwood elves had lived here for centuries, probably doing dignified, weighty sorts of things, but now it was home to dozens of tiny elves who dashed across bridges and scampered through trees and chittered like brightly colored squirrels in a tangle of childish busyness.

Down on the ground, what had once been an open glade was

filled with smaller trees, all that remained of the old Greenwood elves. Years ago, when Rass had first seen them, they'd been a terrifying hybrid of trees and elves. Branches morphing into limbs, agonized faces peering lifelessly out of the bark. But over the past two years, the baby elves had managed to...fix them, climbing around on the trees until the elven parts were somehow soothed. Faces and body parts had slowly faded into the bark, leaving a young, peaceful stand of trees.

"Does Uncle Douglon want a tree?" Rass asked.

Avina nodded, her skin glowing in the dawn light. Her sleeveless dress was a rich green and barely reached her knees, but she showed no sign of being cold. "Doug Doug lub Avina. Avina lub tree." She shrugged. "Doug Doug lub tree."

"There's some sort of logic there." Rass waved to the forest around them. "But Douglon already lives in the trees."

"Doug Doug need *own* tree," Avina said seriously.

"Which one would you give him?"

Avina's brow creased. "No. *Make* one."

"How do you make a tree?"

"Get branch. Put in dirt. Make new tree."

"Oh, a cutting. That's a good idea. Maybe one of the maples? One whose leaves turn red? He likes those."

Avina blinked at her with an appalled look. "Not stupid maple! Vigilant for Doug Doug."

Rass stared at her, then lifted her eyes to where she could see the top of the huge Elder trees towering above the rest of the forest.

The Elder Grove was the seat of power in the woods. Inside, it was a haven of peace, but the Elder trees who guarded it—and they were "whos," not "whats," Rass was sure—were called the Vigilants, and they were terrifying. Their leaves, which never fell, were a malevolent dark green with serrated edges. Along each branch, thick crimson thorns stabbed outward, their tips so sharp they looked as though they could pierce bone.

"How are you going to get a branch of a Vigilant?"

"Vigilant give branch for Doug Doug. Lub Doug Doug."

Rass opened her mouth to object, but Avina's face was set in the determined expression it so often had, and Rass saved her breath. "It takes longer than a fortnight to grow a tree," she pointed out instead.

Avina made an insulted huff and chittered something in elvish, her tone indignant.

Rass raised her hands. "All right! I believe you can do it. What am I going to give him?"

"A tree?"

Rass laughed. "My tree could never compare with yours." She stroked her hand through Avina's hair and looked down the path after Douglon. What did Douglon want?

"Doug Doug lub axe," Avina offered.

"True."

The tiny elf's eyes grew wide, and she looked soberly at Rass. "Avina no touch axe."

"Absolutely not," Rass agreed. "The world is not ready for Avina to have an axe." Douglon did love his axe, but he hardly needed a new one, and she had no idea how to find one anyway. Maybe he could use something else for his axe. Not another whetstone…

She straightened. "A mantel!"

"What is mantel?" Avina asked.

"Dwarves have them." Rass turned and stepped back into the cottage. "In their caves, they have a fireplace, and above that is a shelf, which is the mantel."

Avina looked over at the hole in the dirt floor where a fire was burning. "Mantel go on that?"

"No, that's all wrong." Rass looked around the cottage Douglon had made. His walls were stone, stacked neatly one atop another, his table and chairs were sturdy, made from wood scavenged from around the forest. His fire pit sported a sturdy roasting spit above it.

But there were also a lot of "improvements" made by the tree elves.

Specifically trees.

There were tiny trees growing up in all sorts of places. They wrapped up the corners of the walls, making Douglon swear in dwarvish words Rass didn't know when they loosened his rocks. They grew up too close to the fire pit and were occasionally singed until Douglon threatened to chop them down if some elf didn't move them. They grew up next to the table, restricting the places to sit to just a few awkward gaps.

Rass took it all in, and shook her head. "This is all wrong. Dwarves have mantels over big fireplaces. They put valuable things on it. Douglon's cousin Patlon has a big mantel, and he puts his axe on it."

Avina wrinkled her nose. "Stupid purple axe?"

Rass laughed. "Yes, Patlon's purple axe. Douglon's never said it, but I can tell. He wishes he had a mantel to put his own axe on." She glanced out the door. "He gave up everything to come live with us, you know. No caves, no mantels, no other dwarves."

Avina considered this. "Doug Doug lub Avina," she said, as though that explained everything.

"Yes, that's why he gave it up, because he loves us. Still, I wonder..." Rass looked thoughtfully at the stone walls, an idea forming in her mind.

When Douglon had built their cottage and his workshop, he'd paid dwarves to bring the rock from the Scale Mountains, but there was some stone here in the woods. Maybe enough for what she needed. "I wonder if I could build him a mantel? Can the trees tell you where we can find rock under the ground? I'm going to need a few dwarves, but we'll need rocks too."

Avina ran to one of the larger trees next to the table, setting a hand on it and tilting her head as though listening. "Rock in Rass's clearing."

"I know there's rock there," Rass said. "I can feel it under the grass. Is there more somewhere else? If I build his mantel there, I'll lose my clearing."

Avina shook her head. "No take rocks near trees—Rass hurt trees!"

"It might not hurt the trees," Rass objected, "The rock could be removed carefully, without disturbing the roots too much—"

"No take rocks near trees!"

Rass held up her hands. "All right! So nowhere in the forest except my clearing."

Avina nodded and turned away, apparently bored by the conversation. "Avina make Doug Doug tree!" With a wave, she skipped out the door.

Rass sighed and sank in her chair, wedged between two saplings at the table.

Makes his axe look almost worth having, Douglon had said, nodding his head toward the purple axe on the shelf above the huge fireplace. He'd rolled out a mat of grass for her in front of Patlon's wide hearth, and she'd sat on it, feeling small but warm in the big cave. He'd winked at her. *Must just be the mighty fine mantel it's sitting on.*

They'd sat there all evening around the fire, Douglon and Patlon reminiscing and bantering and drinking ale, Douglon's head thrown back in laughter. The firelight filled the room with flickering light that caught on the axe shaft, making the purple patterns shimmer.

Rass considered the stone cottage again, but there was no room for a mantel here. Nor in his workshop, which was full to the brim with tools and projects, and of course, little saplings.

She stood, pulled her cloak tight, and headed outside, taking the path to her clearing.

When she reached it, she knelt down on the grass.

It was right there, a layer of rock just below the grass that reached nearly to the trees. She stretched her fingers into the stiff, tired blades, feeling their satisfaction in what they were. Content, even with the splendor of summer green long faded. She drew one stalk through her fingers and closed her eyes, thinking of Douglon's face in the firelight.

He was happy here in the woods—she had no doubt of that. When he was here, he laughed often, content in a life he'd certainly never expected.

But in a cave, surrounded by stone and lit by fire...he'd fit so perfectly there.

She opened her eyes and looked over her patch of grass, feeling the carpet of dwindling life, knowing that if she just let it be, come spring, green shoots would squeeze out of the ground like a rising flood of life.

A flood rising over the only stone she could use in the Greenwood.

It couldn't just be a mantel, of course. A mantel was part of a home.

She could imagine it right here, a real dwarven home. A little mountain of rock with a cave. Just what would fit in the clearing. Inside, two small bedrooms and a little living area with a real dwarven fireplace. A fireplace with a mantel to hold Douglon's axe, and set the carved flames on the handle to flickering in the firelight. He'd lean back in his chair, and the room would wrap around him in a way the woods never quite did.

Her hands tightened in the grass, tearing a few blades loose from the earth.

The roots beneath her felt warm and welcoming against her knees. She allowed herself to linger for one more frosty breath, taking in the familiar bumps and dips of her clearing. Running her eyes over the matted spot where she loved to lay.

With a determined nod, she fixed the idea of the mantel in her mind and brushed off her hands. Blinking away a sudden wetness in her eyes, she stood and walked resolutely out of her clearing.

3
THE HELP

RASS STOOD above the basket tucked in the corner of the cottage. She set her hands on her hips, evaluating the collection of red stones. The smallest were tiny specks, the largest tiny pebbles. Not a single one was what she would call big.

They were pretty, she admitted. In a lifeless way.

Douglon had called them rabies or rubies or something and had found them on the Scale Mountains near the edge of the Greenwood. He'd been giddy, chortling about how Patlon would envy the find, how rich this made them. Every one of the forty-six young tree elves and Rass had smiled encouragingly at him, then scampered away to pay attention to living things.

"How many stones do you think it would cost to pay dwarves to help me make the mountain?" she asked Avina.

The little copper elf was kneeling next to the basket, peering into it. "Dwarfies like rocks."

"Yes, they do." Rass reached down and scooped up a big handful, dropping them into a pouch. "Hopefully that will be enough."

Avina wasn't listening. She'd inched her way toward the door with an expression that showed she had somewhere else she'd rather be.

"I'm just going to the nearest door of Duncave," Rass said before Avina could scamper off. "I should be back tomorrow. Please don't cause any trouble while I'm gone."

"No trouble," Avina said seriously. "Avina grow tree for Doug Doug." She ran back to Rass and grabbed her hand, tugging on it until Rass stepped out of the cottage and followed her toward Douglon's workshop.

They turned the corner of the house, and Rass jerked to a stop.

Next to the workshop was a tree barely taller than Rass, yet somehow it loomed.

Darkly.

Rass took a step back.

It was definitely a Vigilant. It had the baleful dark green leaves, their edges as jagged as saw blades. It had the long sharp thorns that glinted blood red among the leaves. Each branch split into thin fingers, almost like grasping, gnarled hands.

But it was also…different.

Its roots wound through a pile of stones before they plunged into the ground, and the rocks seemed to be seeping into the tree itself, tainting the bark with patches of stony grey.

"What did you do?" Rass asked, keeping her voice barely above a whisper, somehow afraid the tree would hear her.

"Dwarfies like rocks." Avina ran up to the terrifying tree and crawled over its roots, deftly fitting her bare feet between the thorns that grew even there. "Avina put rock in Vigilant." She smiled proudly up at Rass. "Teach tree to drink rock."

Rass moved cautiously forward and touched the nearest branch, feeling the bark between two thorns. It felt like stone.

"Avina," she said slowly, "this is amazing. But…the wood is so unique that Douglon is going to want to build things from it."

Avina gave her a bright nod. "Tree lub Doug Doug. Will give him branches."

Rass backed away, wiping off her fingers as though something poisonous might have oozed out of the bark. "If you say so."

Avina swung herself up onto the lowest branch, dancing around

18

the thorns until she settled into a little crook in the wood. "Tree lub Avina, too."

"Of course it does."

The tiny elf set her hands on the bark and closed her eyes.

Rass glanced up at the sky. "I need to go. Don't you or your tree cause any trouble."

Avina waved a copper hand at her in a shooing motion.

Rass glanced around the nearby trees, seeing elven faces watching her. "Don't any of you cause trouble."

The grins she got back weren't reassuring, but she didn't have time to worry about them.

It turned out she did have time to worry. A lot of time.

The dwarves had begun to guard a door close to the Greenwood, since the High Dwarf Patlon often called Douglon to the caves, but the walk to the entrance of the dwarven realm was still more than half a day's walk. And that was during the summer months when the grass and Rass were strong and sturdy. Now, as she stepped through the brittle frosty brush covering the ground, her steps felt small and slow, and she found herself fretting about the young elves merely because it was better than fretting about her clearing.

Her path led uphill to the feet of the Scale Mountains, and the higher she climbed, the colder the air grew. A wind whipped out of the north, grasping at her cloak and chilling her gaunt cheeks. Her fingers went from cold to numb, and her boots dragged over the rough ground.

It was late afternoon when she finally reached the door, which looked like nothing more than another rock in a rocky cliff face. She picked up a stone, which felt surprisingly heavy, and rapped three times.

The noise was insignificant, but she waited a breath and rapped again.

A shuffling noise came through the door, and part of the cliff shifted, revealing a crack, darkness, and a sliver of a shaggy dwarven head.

"Rass?" The door was shoved open a bit wider, and Gunner, one of the few dwarves she recognized, stepped into view. He took in her sunken appearance, and his eyes widened. "What's wrong?"

Three more dwarves peered over his shoulders from behind him, and she was relieved to see she knew all but one.

"Nothing's wrong. I need some help on a job. A present. For Douglon."

Gunner raised an eyebrow. "Does Douglon know you look like you're about to collapse?"

She gave him a weak smile. "This is what I look like every winter. He knows."

He considered the words, then nodded somewhat reluctantly. "What sort of help do you need?"

"I want to build him a mantel," Rass said. "In the Greenwood."

The four dwarves looked at her with varying levels of amusement.

"I have stone," she added. "I just need some dwarves because...I don't know how to build a mantel."

"You mean a hearth? A fireplace and a place to sit?"

Rass paused. "A mantel. For him to put his axe on."

"Ahh," he said. "An axe does look nice on a mantel." He stroked his long black beard and squinted at her. "Well, a mantel should be inside a room, not a forest."

Rass let out a tired sigh and leaned her shoulder against the nearest rock. "Yes, you'll need to build a cave around it. A whole mountain, actually, but the mantel is the important part. And I need it done before Midwinter when Douglon will be back."

"A mountain?"

"A little mountain. In a little clearing."

"We can't just leave our post," Gunner said kindly. "We have important things to—"

"You sit in there and drink your smelly ale," she interrupted, "and play cards because no one besides Douglon ever comes to this door."

"That's not entirely tru—"

She grabbed Gunner's huge hand with her own small one and dumped the pouch of rubies out into it. "I can pay you."

Gunner stared at the uncut gems with his mouth half-open. The other three craned to see over his shoulders, equally stunned.

"Three of us can come with you for a bit and build a mantel," Gunner said, closing his fingers around the gems.

"And a mountain," Rass prompted.

"Sure, a mountain too," Gunner said. "C'mon, boys. Let's grab some tools. The little elf needs some help."

4

THE GIVING AND THE GIFT

CLAIMING RASS WALKED TOO SLOW, Gunner lifted her up to ride on his broad shoulder for the trip back to the Greenwood, and at the dwarves' quick pace, they arrived before dark. Rass hopped down and led them to her clearing. The glade was peaceful and quiet in the dusky light. The orange hue of the clouds overhead made the dried grass glow with a warmth that called to Rass, and she stepped into it, clasping her hands together to keep them from shaking.

Avina chittered at them from a low branch, watching the dwarves curiously.

Gunner smiled up at her. "Hello there, little cutie!" He reached a hand toward her.

She drew her lips back in a snarl, revealing a dozen sharp, pointy teeth.

He snatched his arm back. "Is she safe?" he asked Rass.

"Most of the time." Rass faced the dwarves. Clearing her throat, she tried to keep her voice steady. "There's rock just under the grass in this whole area. Will that be enough? For a small mountain with a cave? And a mantel?"

Gunner stepped onto the grass, slid a pickaxe off his back, and swung it in a wide arc.

The tip stabbed into the earth, and Rass flinched. It sank in a handbreadth, then clanged against rock.

"Should be easy enough," Gunner said. "The slow part will be pulling the rock up. Once that's done, the building will be easy."

"Trees can pull up rock," Avina said brightly.

She set her palm on the trunk next to her, and the tree shuddered. Then the one beside it. Then the next. In a breath, the entire clearing was surrounded by quivering trees.

The earth under Rass's feet trembled, and slowly a thick ring of ground around the clearing began to rise.

The dwarves swore and staggered back. Rass moved away from the trees into the center of the grass, spinning as deep cracks reverberated underfoot.

She choked back a cry as the roots of the grass were ripped apart, the surface of her clearing roiling and seething. Thick chunks of stone emerged from the earth, toppling over and crushing the dried grass.

When the rumbling stopped and the ground stilled, Avina stood proudly on her branch, surveying her work.

The clearing had been churned up, the slab of stone that had lain underground now split and exposed on the surface, the blanket of grass torn and smashed and ravaged.

Rass stood on a tiny island of grass. All around her was nothing but devastation.

She turned away from the dwarves and Avina, her arms wrapped around her stomach, trying to catch her breath around a sob rising in her throat.

She squeezed her eyes shut, focusing on Douglon by the hearth. She swallowed and forced her arms to loosen. There was more grass in other places. She could always find more grass.

She turned back to the dwarves, who were moving warily closer. "Will this work?" The words came out trembly, but she squeezed her hands into determined fists. "Is this enough space?" she asked more firmly. "And enough rock?"

"This is perfect," Gunner said slowly, glancing at the trees. "Are they done moving?"

"Trees done," Avina said. "Dwarfies make Doug Doug mantel."

Gunner nodded. "Let's get to work, boys. We can do a bit before we lose all the light."

There was a small patch of grass undisturbed along the side of the clearing, just large enough for Rass to sit on the next morning. She pulled her knees up to her chest and watched the dwarves split and roll and stack stones, starting the edges of a small mountain peak that filled the clearing.

The morning was even colder than yesterday. Her nose was constantly cold, and her fingers had a hard time holding her cloak tightly enough around herself to stay warm.

But she wanted to stay. Needed to stay and watch her clearing.

Before many hours had passed, the grass that had poked out between upturned rocks had been torn up by the heavy tread of dwarven boots and the rolling of stones.

Rass allowed herself a few tears as the last of the blades were trampled before rubbing her face dry and watching with interest.

Over the next few days, the rocks were pulled from the ground, lowering the entire clearing a bit as sides of a mountain grew up, rising like a rocky peak. It was up to the dwarves' shoulders before they began working on the hollow inside.

Two tiny bedrooms were tucked on the outside edges before they started on the main room. The fireplace and mantel sprouted up stone by stone. Gunner called for slight changes or chiseling off some offending spur of rock. It was smaller than Patlon's mantel, but it fit well inside the cave, and was large enough to hold Douglon's axe, which was all that mattered.

For eight days, the clearing rang with the sound of chisels and hammers and dwarven songs. Dozens of tree elves hung from the surrounding branches, stopping by to see the odd sight, and Rass watched it all, wrapped in her new cloak, nodding to herself with each bit of work done. The more it grew, the more she could picture him there, sitting by that fire, his feet stretched out toward the flames.

It was only at night, when the tree elves had finally fallen asleep and the dwarves were snoring loudly, that the pang of loss shadowed her thoughts.

The ninth day, Rass spent the morning foraging through the forest for tall grass and the afternoon weaving it together into a mat. A little before dinner, Gunner came over to her, brushing off his hands.

"Would you like to see it?" he asked with a broad smile.

She jumped up with her mat and followed the broad dwarf down the path.

They came around the last bend in the path, and the miniature mountain peak sat in front of them, rising up half as tall as the trees. It was rocky and jagged and perfect. Like the top of some lofty pinnacle seen from afar. Gunner led her down a little path of flat rocks running from the forest to the arched front door and motioned for her to enter.

And…it was exactly like stepping into a mountain. A minuscule mountain. A mountain even she could stride across with a handful of steps. But a real mountain nevertheless.

The main room was round, with stone walls arching up to meet overhead. Straight ahead, a fireplace as wide as Rass's outstretched arms opened in the back wall, a chimney rising above it made of huge stalwart blocks of rock. It was steady and solid and welcoming.

A fire burned in the fireplace, its light cheery and its crackle like a fiery chuckle.

Above it, on the mantel, sat a carved stand, precisely positioned to hold an axe.

"It's perfect," she breathed.

She moved to the entryway and set her mat carefully on the flat stones that had been cut to fit neatly in the floor.

Gunner handed her the pouch she'd paid him with, still half-full of rubies. "You paid us too much, little one. Douglon would skin me alive if he knew I'd taken so much from you."

Rass took the pouch and clutched it to her chest, spinning again and taking in the new space. There wasn't enough grass, of course, but there never was. And this was a happy place. A homey place.

A perfectly dwarvish homey home.

"Thank you," she whispered.

5

THE LONGEST NIGHT

Rᴀss ᴅʀᴀɢɢᴇᴅ the chair along the path, its two back legs bumping and jouncing over rocks. Her fingers ached at having to grip it, her legs felt heavy and clumsy, and her breath puffed out in quick clouds. The sky had been low and heavy all day, and though the wind gusting down from the north had an icy bite to it, she'd taken her woolen cloak off hours ago.

But this chair was the last thing.

After the dwarves had left this morning, she'd spent the entire day bringing things from Douglon's workshop and the cottage to the clearing.

No, not the clearing, she reminded herself, tugging the chair that seemed to grow heavier and more unwieldy with each step. *The mountain.*

She'd brought over a selection of whetstones Douglon liked to use in the evening hours to sharpen his tools. Especially the one reserved for his axe and the new one from Alaric. She'd brought over one of the lanterns and some oil, the smaller of their sheepskin rugs, the smaller of their kettles, and a mismatched pair of clay mugs. She'd woven two more grass mats to put on the floor, softening the stones a bit in front of each chair, and turned an old stool into a table for the corner with a basin for water.

They'd need to bring over bedding and Douglon's big mattress and Rass's small one full of fuzzy wool that he'd bought last year, but those would take dwarf strength, not winter-grass-elf strength.

She pulled on the chair wearily, one of its legs gouging into the dirt just outside the cave until she finally tugged it onto the stone floor and dragged it to the side of the hearth, facing the other chair.

When it was in place, she collapsed into it, letting her head fall back and closing her eyes. Her arms hung limply in her lap. The quiet of the world around her settled into the room, and her breathing slowed and quieted. Ignoring the cold, she kicked off the winter boots Douglon had given her and slouched down until she could wriggle her toes on the grass mat at her feet.

She opened her eyes and looked around the room wearily. The things she'd brought weren't perfect. The chairs were mismatched, the stool with the water basin listed a bit to the side...

"Rass!" Avina's voice jolted her awake as the little elf shook her shoulder. "Rass! Trees say Doug Doug in forest! Come! Come! Give Doug Doug gifts!"

Rass rubbed her face, but even lifting her hand felt heavy. The world had darkened while she slept, and the air had grown frigid. Through the arched doorway, thick snowflakes floated down, coating the ground in white. "How long has it been snowing?"

Avina glanced out the door. "Since it started." She skipped back and forth from the chair to the door while Rass fumbled with her boots. Her fingers were too cold to work the laces well, and her feet felt like ice.

"Hurry!" Avina prodded her.

Rass finished with her boots and heaved herself out of the chair. She pinned her cloak on and glanced around the hearth, suddenly nervous.

"Rass!" Avina cried. "Come!"

"One last thing." The cave was already full of shadows, so Rass lit the lantern, setting it on the table next to Douglon's chair so that it cast a soft golden light over the fireplace and the mantel.

The light transformed the room into a cozy chamber, and she nodded. "It's not perfect," she whispered to herself, "but I think he'll like it."

She stepped outside into a world of white. The torn-up ground around the edge of the clearing was covered with a layer of snow, smoothing the edges of sharp rocks and blanketing the churned earth into soft mounds.

Avina skipped ahead, still barefoot and bare armed. The white flakes that drifted down to land on her melted and rose away in strands of mist as she chattered about Douglon's approach.

Rass pulled the hood of her cloak up, reveling in the warmth that it held around her neck.

Before they reached the Nursery, she heard the other elves hooting and laughing and chittering at each other like squirrels.

The bridges and ropes high in the trees were filled with scurrying elves and puffs of thrown snow. They were scooping it into piles on the platforms that weren't under the canopy, or they were racing around on the ground, grabbing it by the handful and flinging it at each other.

The glee of the tree elves filled the Nursery with a brightness that Rass could almost see, and she found herself smiling up at them.

Avina, though, peered down the path winding into the woods, flitting from one tree to the next. "Doug Doug close!" she called over her shoulder.

Moments later, there was a glimpse of motion down the path and a flash of red from his axe handle, and Avina whooped and raced toward him, leaping into the air and throwing herself into his arms.

Rass stood outside their stone cottage, gripping her cloak close around her.

"Present!" Avina squealed when Douglon had carried her into the Nursery. She squirmed down from his arms. He held a sack in one hand, bulging with something vaguely rounded, so she grabbed his other hand and tugged him forward.

"Yes, I have a present for you," Douglon said to her, jiggling the sack.

This brought her up short, and she stopped, biting her lip and considering the mysterious bundle.

Douglon took in all the elves frolicking in the snow. They called out greetings to him, and he gave them waves. "I have a present for all of you," he shouted over their noise.

Squeals and shouts met this announcement as the other forty-five tree elves swung and leapt and tumbled toward him, their colored hair and skin like a tide of jewels and autumn leaves swirling over the snowy ground.

He glanced at Rass over the brightly colored heads and gave her a grin. "Hello, snip!" His gaze traveled to the sharp edges of her shoulders and the thin fingers holding her cloak closed. "You still exist under that thick cloak, right? You haven't quite wasted away to nothing while I was gone?" His words were light, but there was a hint of real worry in his eyes.

The entire wood felt better with him here. Safer. More homey. She loosened her grip on her cloak and smiled at him. "Not quite yet. Welcome home, Uncle."

"Rass fine," Avina said with an air of reproof.

"Of course she is." Douglon held the sack up, out of reach of the elves. "She's the strongest, bravest grass elf in the world. Now to the stream, you little horde of monsters. To the stream!"

Like a school of fish, the elves shifted directions and poured toward the spring that flowed nearby, the water nearly black next to the white snow. He knelt down, setting his sack beside it, patting heads and taking kisses on his bearded cheek, then held his hands up for silence. With a great amount of difficulty and a great amount of jostling, they stilled.

"Today is Midwinter," he began. "It's the time of the year when we have the shortest day and the most darkness."

Rass stepped up to the edge of the crowd, looking curiously at his lumpy bag.

"Last year, you all were too young"—he glanced around at them all with a pointed look—"too much like tiny colored bundles of mayhem and madness to understand, but this year, I think you're big enough."

An elf with spiky blue hair reached up and grabbed the bottom of Douglon's beard.

He winced and gently untangled the fingers. "Both humans and dwarves give gifts to those they love on this day. The humans call them Candlelight Gifts and say a good gift brings light on the darkest night, like a candle flame. Since, in ways I never would have expected and still can't fully understand, I happen to love all you wild monsters very deeply, I wanted to give you a gift."

He untied the top of the sack and scooted the canvas down, revealing a wooden wheel. "This is a water wheel." The contraption only came to his knees, and the elves shoved against each other to see it better. Legs folded out from the sides and stretched to either side of the stream. Douglon made a few adjustments until the bottom of the wheel dipped into the water, and it began to spin.

Buckets along the rim scooped up water, lifting it high until they flipped over and dumped it back into the stream.

Rass clapped with the other elves who cheered and pushed closer.

"Water wheels can do all sorts of useful things," Douglon continued, rummaging in the sack and bringing out a few more lengths of wood. "But you elves don't care about usefulness, so I had this one made to be as silly as you are."

He attached a curved wooden channel to one side where it would catch the water from the buckets. It wasn't entirely smooth, and when the stream of water started down it, it frothed and roiled over bumps before turning a corner and falling right back into the stream. More oohs and clapping greeted this development, but they all fell silent when Douglon unwrapped a final bundle and a jingle rang out.

The final piece sat over the channel, where it dangled a half-dozen chains into the water. The first two had bells attached to them, and the turbulent water set them to dancing, ringing like a tiny festival. The second two chains held wooden shapes that struck each other when the water jostled them, letting out a chorus of knocking noises, little drums beating out a merry cadence beneath the tinkling of the bells.

The final two chains held metal gates that hung down, making the water tumble and squeeze around them until it burbled with a sound like laughter.

When all the chains were situated, the water flowed through the contraption, sending out jingles and chimes and knocks and gurgles like a crowd of fairies at a celebration.

The forty-six elves jumped up and laughed and cheered and danced. Douglon backed up, looking pleased. Rass came to stand next to him, leaning her shoulder against his arm. "It sounds like all of them!"

He grinned. "That's what I thought too." He nudged her shoulder. "I have a gift for you too, snip."

Avina looked up at his words. "Gift!" She grabbed Douglon's hand again. "Gift for Doug Doug!"

"For me?" He glanced at Rass.

"I have something for you too," Rass said quietly. "But you should see Avina's first." She couldn't quite keep the grimace off her face, and a wrinkle of concern formed between Douglon's brows.

When Avina led him around the side of the stone cottage, he jerked to a stop and swore, throwing out an arm to protect Rass.

The Vigilant was now taller than Douglon's shop. The trunk was nearly as wide as the dwarf himself, the bark a sharp stony grey with grooves of deep black. The dark green leaves were shiny, their edges jagged. The snow gathered on them somehow only accentuated the knife-like points. The thorns seemed even longer than those on the other Elder trees, too. Deeper red and more brooding. They jabbed from between branches and out of the trunk as though the tree held a thousand vicious blades.

The ends of the branches twitched toward them, sending snow tumbling off, and Douglon tensed.

"Tree for Doug Doug!" Avina beamed up at him.

"Avina grew you an Elder tree," Rass said, trying to keep her voice cheerful as she fought the urge to take a step back. "And then somehow fed it some rocks so the bark turned…" She gestured to the tree. "Like that," she finished weakly.

"It's...uh..." Douglon looked down at Avina and tried to smile. "It's very ferocious."

"Like Doug Doug," Avina said proudly, running up to the trunk and patting it between the thorns.

Douglon reached for her, as though he could pull her back from the spines.

"Avina says the Vigilants love you," Rass said, staying close to Douglon, "and that this one will give you branches to use that will be as hard as stone."

"That's..." Douglon swallowed.

"Doug Doug like?" Avina asked expectantly.

Douglon focused on her. "I love it, Avina. You must have worked very hard to grow it so fast."

She smiled shyly. "Avina and trees lub Doug Doug."

He took a step toward her, looking warily up at the branches, but the tree stayed still while he reached the tiny elf and carefully pulled her into a hug, away from the thorns. He kept his eyes up on the branches. "I love you too, Avina. Thank you for my tree."

The other elves had started some game with the water wheel, and Avina, after pecking Douglon's cheek with a kiss, wriggled out of his arms and ran to join them.

Douglon backed away slowly, still watching the tree. One of the branches dipped toward him, and he flinched back. "Uh..."

"I know," Rass said.

The snow fell gently and silently onto the Vigilant, each addition of white somehow making the tree look more dangerous.

Douglon shifted, and the red handle of his axe sticking out the top of his pack shimmered against the white snow all around them. Rass dragged her attention away from the tree. If Douglon went into either the cottage or his workshop to put the pack down, he'd notice all the things she'd taken to furnish the mountain.

"Can I give you your gift?" Rass said.

One eyebrow raised, and he gave her a sidelong look. "Did you make me tall frightening grass?"

She laughed. "Maybe next year. Come to my clear—" She stopped. "Come this way."

He paused, and she readied herself to tell him that he couldn't put his pack away, but he just shifted it on his shoulders and nodded.

"I didn't know the Vigilants could get more frightening, but somehow she managed," Rass said as they started down the path.

Douglon glanced back at the tree once more before it disappeared from view. "It's both terrifying and intriguing. Sort of like Avina herself."

Rass smiled, her eyes searching ahead through the forest, looking for the first glimpse of stone, but the snow was falling fast now, and the light was fading. "Did you go to Duncave just to pick up the water wheel?"

"That was part of the reason. I commissioned it a couple of months ago, but it took ages for them to complete it."

"That shouldn't have taken a fortnight. What else did you do?"

He gave her a mischievous smile. "You'll see."

They walked in silence for a few minutes. The noises of the Nursery had faded to distant hoots and squeals, and the sound of their footsteps was muffled by the snow. They reached the final curve, and Rass gripped the warm fabric of her cloak in her hands, her stomach twisting in nervousness or excitement—she couldn't decide which.

She caught a glimpse of the lantern light and a bit of stone. She looked up at him and saw him peering curiously toward the light.

They turned the last corner, the mountain came into view, and Douglon stumbled to a stop.

6

THE CANDLELIGHT GIFTS

DOUGLON JUST STOOD THERE, snow falling onto his hair and beard, gathering on his shoulders as he stared at the mountain, his mouth hanging open.

In the gathering dusk, the peak stood covered with a soft layer of white. The bit of clearing left was similarly blanketed. The stone path, which hadn't gathered snow as quickly as the earth around it, was like a miniature valley winding toward the arched doorway. Inside, the lantern burned merry and bright in the growing night.

The light lit the stones of the fireplace and the mantel. It warmed the wooden angles of the chairs and glittered on the bits of snow that had landed on Rass's welcome mat just inside the door.

Rass looked up at him, her hands clutched at her chest, waiting for his reaction.

His eyes dropped down to hers, and he sank down to his knees, oblivious to the snow.

There was an expression in his eyes that Rass couldn't decipher, and she gripped her cloak tighter. It wasn't anger or even shock. Not disappointment or disapproval or any of the reactions she'd been preparing herself for. He simply stared at her with a peculiar look.

"Your clearing's gone," he whispered, as though his mind was still trying to make sense of his own words.

There was something woven into the complexity of his expression. Something deep and anguished. Something that recognized the depth of her loss in a way she hadn't even let herself face. Her throat tightened against rising tears.

"I built you a mantel," she managed to whisper back.

Douglon looked back at the mountain, then at the thin strip of clearing left around it. "Your clearing is gone," he repeated, this time almost with an air of bewilderment.

Rass reached out for his shoulder but hesitated with her hand outstretched. "There's other grass," she said, her voice small. "I built you a mantel for your axe, like dwarves have. We can sit and talk by the fire."

He turned slowly back to her. "You built me a mantel?"

"Well, I paid some dwarves to build it." She forced one corner of her mouth up into a smile. "And the home around it. A real dwarven home. I thought you would like it. I thought you would like a place to put your axe."

He let out a huff of something between a laugh and a sob and wrapped his arms around her shoulders.

She leaned in against him, pressing her face into his neck. The cold prick of the snow against her skin dissolved immediately against his warmth.

"You built a mantel for my axe." His words were rough, and she felt him let out another pained laugh. "You gave up your clearing for that?"

She nodded against him, adding her tears to the melting snow. "I'd give up all the clearings in the world for you, Uncle."

He pulled back, his eyes wet. "That would probably kill you," he pointed out.

She sniffed. "You'd find a way to keep me alive."

"I would." He hugged her tightly again. "No matter what it took."

His arms covered half her back. He sniffed, then let out a breath, this one almost sorrowful. She drew back to look at him, a sharp fear coursing through her. "You don't like it."

He chuckled, a strange sound that was too strangled to be happy, and looked at her with a helpless sort of expression. "I have never loved a gift more. But..." He brushed some snow off her hair and shook his head.

"It's not sad," she assured him. "There's other grass. I can find lots of places to lie. I wanted to give you this, and the clearing was the right place for it. The place with rock. The trees helped push the stone up, and the dwarves built it for me and it turned into a beautiful mountain and—"

He dropped his hand to her shoulder. "I'm not sad. Not exactly. Or not totally." He shook his head. "Let's go inside and start a fire, and I'll show you."

They stepped inside, and she clasped her arms around herself again as she watched his face. He took in the walls and the chairs and the fireplace. He peered into the two small bedrooms. He noted the grass mats and smiled with enough genuine happiness that she let herself relax slightly and climb into her own chair.

The dwarves had stacked wood near the fireplace, and it was the work of a few moments for Douglon to get a fire started. When he did, he knelt there for an extra moment, looking up at the shelf and the stand for his axe.

"Put it up there," Rass said. "Let's see how it looks."

"Soon enough," he said gently. "First, your gift." From his pack, he brought out a leather pouch dyed light green like spring grass and handed it to her. Then he sank into his chair. "Open it."

She untied the string and reached inside.

Her fingers touched seeds.

Thousands of seeds.

Seeds she recognized.

She drew in a sharp breath and pulled out a handful.

Grass seed from the Sweep.

Blades of grass that would grow as tall as her, wave in the wind like a rippling ocean.

She stared up at him. "How...?"

"I didn't just go to Duncave. I went over to the Sweep." He stretched his feet toward the slowly growing fire, watching her.

The seeds were smooth, and she let them run through her fingers almost like water. "It'll grow so tall! We'll spread it when the snow melts, and by early summer the whole clearing will be—"

Her hand closed around the remaining seeds, the sharp ends stabbing into her palm, but not as sharp as the jab of dismay in her heart.

She raised her eyes slowly to meet his. "Oh," she said quietly. "My clearing is gone."

He rested his head onto the tall back of the chair, the side of his mouth curling up in a smile she couldn't quite understand. "Not a problem I expected. I wondered if your clearing was large enough, if our soil was right, if it was deep enough for the roots." His eyes ran over the walls of his cave. "But I did not account for this."

Rass let the seed fall back into the pouch and tied it up securely and took a deep breath. "We'll figure something out," she said, keeping her voice steady. "We'll plant it around the edges of the mountain, or near the Nursery, or…we'll find something." She caught sight of him looking at the mantel, an inexplicable sorrow in his eyes, and felt a stab of guilt.

She flung the pouch on the table by the lantern and rushed to his chair, throwing her arms around his neck. "But I love it! I can't believe you went so far! How did you do it so quickly? It's the greatest gift I could ever imagine!"

She blanketed his cheek with kisses.

"It's all right, snip," he said, patting her back. "It's all right."

She backed up and smiled widely at him. "Truly. I love it. Now, put your axe up on the mantel so we can see how it looks."

At her words, he ran his hand through his beard, a small smile growing to a larger one, and then a laugh rolled out of him, starting out helpless, then turning richer.

"What's wrong? Don't you want to see how it looks?"

Still laughing, he reached down and grasped the handle of his axe, which, she realized, was sticking out of the top of his pack instead of buckled to the outside like usual.

It slid out effortlessly until he held a shaft of wood, decorated with red flames and with no axe blade at all.

Rass stared at the empty end of the shaft.

"I sold the blade to buy your seeds," he said with another chuckle.

"Sold? But..." She looked at his face, trying to see if he was making some joke. "But we have rubies."

"Who would have imagined that grass seed would cost rubies?" he said, standing. "I took some coins with me, but there were fires along the Sweep this summer, the whole eastern side was burned. The price of grass seed is sky high." He set the handle up on the mantel, leaning it on the stand. It didn't fit right without the heavy blade and left the mantel looking unfinished. Unbalanced.

Douglon adjusted the wooden handle in vain, finally just letting it sit awkwardly against the stand.

"You sold your stonesteel blade?" she asked in a whisper. "For me?"

He turned and knelt in front of her, still smiling. "Of course I did. I never wanted a family, you know. Had no idea what I was missing. Never imagined one could make me as happy as you do, little snip." He enclosed her once more in a hug, and she breathed in the scent of leather.

"I'm glad you're home, Uncle," she said into his shoulder.

"So am I."

He straightened and looked around the cave fondly. "In the whole history of the world, there may not ever have been two better Candlelight Gifts."

Rass dashed away the last of her tears and smiled. "Well, no family has ever loved each other more."

He kissed her forehead, his beard tickling her face. "I think that's true."

The world had darkened to a deep blue. Drifting snowflakes caught the firelight outside the door and glinted like bits of magic floating through the air.

The fire popped, and Douglon picked up another log to add to it. "When dwarves move into a new cave, it's their first meal that makes it officially home. If you put the kettle on, I'll find us something to eat, and we'll spend the first of many hours by the hearth. I'll tell you all about the Sweep, and you can tell me how Avina managed to combine a tree with a rock."

Rass picked up the pouch of seeds and hugged it to her chest. The firelight and the sparkles of snow held back the growing darkness of the night. Douglon fiddled with the hook for the kettle, humming in approval at the work the other dwarves had done, and Rass stood in her little world of warmth.

Stretching up on her tiptoes, she set the pouch of seeds carefully next to Douglon's axe handle. It was no axe blade, but there was something pleasing about how it looked.

She smiled up at it before turning to find and fill the kettle.

The night grew black outside, the wind blustered, and the snow fell in drifts, but the two of them sat snugly and chatted inside their cave, which glowed like a candle flame in the darkness.

THE END

AUTHOR'S NOTE

Thank you for reading The Candlelight Gifts! I hope you enjoyed this little snippet about Douglon and Rass.

If this is your first encounter with those two characters, and the lines "Down on the ground, what had once been an open glade was filled with smaller trees, all that remained of the old Greenwood elves. Years ago, when Rass had first seen them, they'd been a terrifying hybrid of trees and elves. Branches morphing into limbs, agonized faces peering lifelessly out of the bark." made no sense to you, you can find that entire story in The Keeper Chronicles on Amazon, or on Audible narrated by Tim Gerard Reynolds.

You can find a list of all my books and a suggested reading order at www.jaandrews.com/books.

To be notified when new books are published (and get a free short story), you can sign up for JA Andrews' newsletter and get another free short story on her website at jaandrews.com/ghost

Made in the USA
Middletown, DE
30 October 2023

41491988R00033